ERIC CARLE

The Greedy Python

Written by Richard Buckley

LITTLE SIMON

New York   London   Toronto   Sydney   New Delhi

Half hidden in the jungle green
The biggest snake there's ever been
Wound back and forth and in between.

The giant snake was very strong
And very, very, very long.
He had a monstrous appetite,
His stomach stretched from left to right.

He quickly gobbled in one bite
Whatever creatures came in sight:
A mouse that scampered to and fro,
A frog that jumped up from below,
A bat that hung from his left toe,
A fish that swam a bit too slow,
A bird that flew a bit too low,

A porcupine still half asleep,
A monkey who was in mid-leap,

A leopard sitting in a tree,
A buffalo who came to see.

An elephant, complete with trunk,
Was swallowed in a single chunk.
"I'm far too big to eat!" he cried.
"Oh, no you're not!" the snake replied.

At last the python's meal was done
And he lay resting in the sun.
The animals inside his skin
Were making quite a dreadful din;

And when they all began to kick,
The snake began to feel quite sick.

He coughed the whole lot up again—
Each one of them—and there were ten.

He soon felt better, and what's more
Was hungrier than just before.
He hadn't learned a single thing:
His greed was quite astonishing.
He saw his own tail, long and curved,
And thought that lunch was being served.

He closed his jaws on his own rear
Then swallowed hard . . . and disappeared!

 LITTLE SIMON

An imprint of Simon & Schuster Children's Publishing Division

1230 Avenue of the Americas, New York, New York 10020

First Little Simon book and CD edition May 2015

Text copyright © 1985 by Richard Buckley

Illustrations copyright © 1985 by Eric Carle

Originally published by Picture Book Studio 1985

Also available in a Little Simon board book edition

For information about special discounts for bulk purchases, please contact Simon & Schuster Special Sales at 1-866-506-1949 or business@simonandschuster.com.

The Simon & Schuster Speakers Bureau can bring authors to your live event. For more information or to book an event contact the Simon & Schuster Speakers Bureau at 1-866-248-3049 or visit our website at www.simonspeakers.com.

Manufactured in China 0215 SCP

10 9 8 7 6 5 4 3 2 1

ISBN 978-1-4814-1959-8

Eric Carle was born in Syracuse, New York, and moved to Germany with his parents when he was six years old. He studied at the Academy of Graphic Arts in Stuttgart before returning to the United States, where he worked as a graphic designer for the *New York Times* and later as art director for an international advertising agency. His first two books, *1, 2, 3 to the Zoo* and *The Very Hungry Caterpillar*, gained him immediate international recognition. The latter title, now considered a modern classic, has sold more than thirty million copies and has been translated into forty-eight languages. Eric Carle and his wife, Barbara, divide their time between the mountains of North Carolina and the Florida Keys.

Richard Buckley is a much-traveled English writer of both prose and poetry. He has lived in New York, Paris, and London, but his present home is in Cheltenham, England, where he has lived for the past thirty years, bringing up two sons with his wife (and muse), Elfie. His books for children include *The Dutiful Penguin*, *The Foolish Tortoise* (with Eric Carle), and *The Bird Who Couldn't Fly* (with Alex Williams).